SENTINEL

Story: **Sean McKeever**

Pencils and Inks: **UDON with Eric Vedder, Joe Vriens, & Scott Hepburn**

Colors: **UDON**   UDON Chief: **Erik Ko**   Letters: **Cory Petit**

Assistant Editor: **Andy Schmidt**   Editor: **Marc Sumerak**   Editor in Chief: **Joe Quesada**

President: **Bill Jemas**

DISCOVERY

Part 2

VISIT US AT
www.abdopublishing.com

Reinforced library bound edition published in 2007 by Spotlight, a division of the ABDO Publishing Group, Edina, Minnesota. Spotlight produces high-quality reinforced library bound editions for schools and libraries. Published by agreement with Marvel Characters, Inc.

Library of Congress Cataloging-in-Publication Data

McKeever, Sean.
    Sentinel / [story, Sean McKeever ; pencils and inks, UDON ... et al.].
      v. cm.
    Cover title.
    Revisions of issues 1-6 of the serial Sentinel.
    "Marvel Age."
    Contents: #1. Salvage -- #2. Discovery -- #3. Pet project -- #4. Rebuilding -- #5. Test mission -- #6. Primary targets.
    ISBN-13: 978-1-59961-316-1 (v. 1)
    ISBN-10: 1-59961-316-6 (v. 1)
    ISBN-13: 978-1-59961-317-8 (v. 2)
    ISBN-10: 1-59961-317-4 (v. 2)
    ISBN-13: 978-1-59961-318-5 (v. 3)
    ISBN-10: 1-59961-318-2 (v. 3)
    ISBN-13: 978-1-59961-319-2 (v. 4)
    ISBN-10: 1-59961-319-0 (v. 4)
    ISBN-13: 978-1-59961-320-8 (v. 5)
    ISBN-10: 1-59961-320-4 (v. 5)
    ISBN-13: 978-1-59961-321-5 (v. 6)
    ISBN-10: 1-59961-321-2 (v. 6)
    1. Comic books, strips, etc. I. UDON. II. Title. III. Title: Salvage. IV. Title: Discovery. V. Title: Pet project. VI. Title: Rebuilding. VII. Title: Test mission. VIII. Title: Primary targets.

PN6728.S453 M35 2007
741.5'973--dc22

                2006050623

All Spotlight books are reinforced library binding
and manufactured in the United States of America.

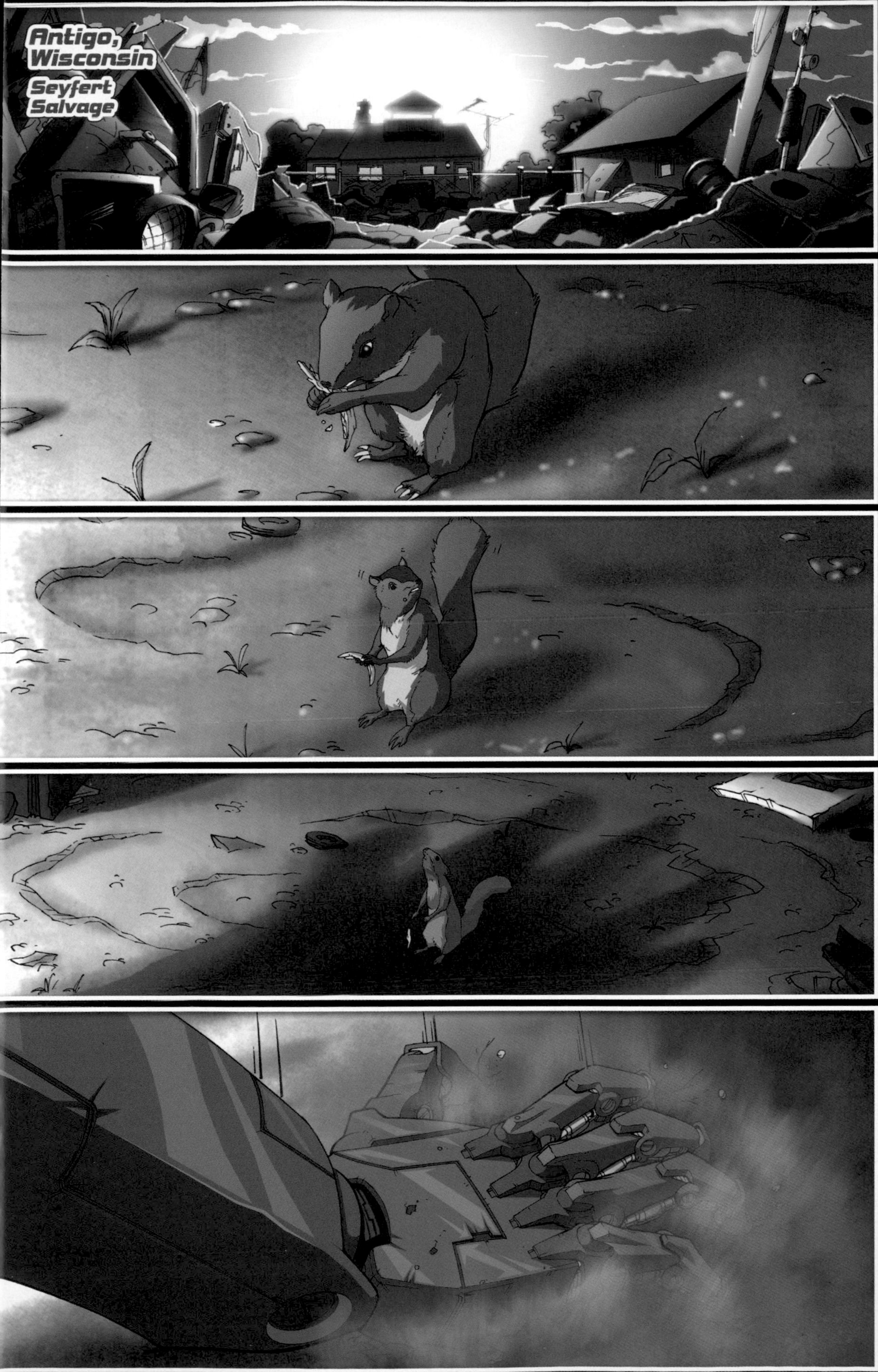
Antigo, Wisconsin
Seyfert Salvage

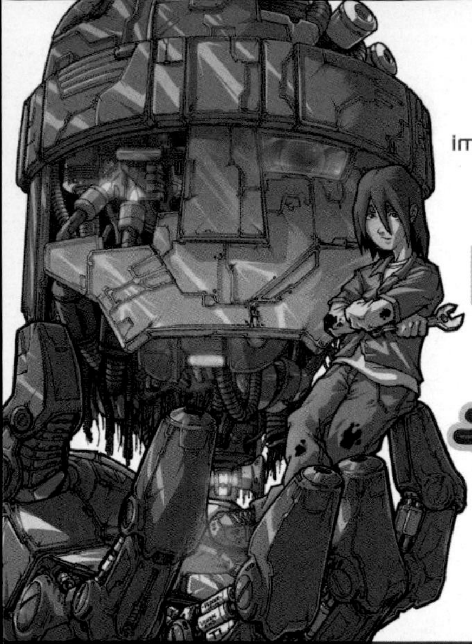

Juston Seyfert is about to make the discovery of a lifetime: the damaged remains of a 30-foot-tall robot, buried in his father's junkyard! But will his impending discovery lead to the birth of a new hero...or to unbridled revenge for a life full of hardships...? Stan Lee Presents:

SENTINEL

"SALVAGE"
part 2

Previously...

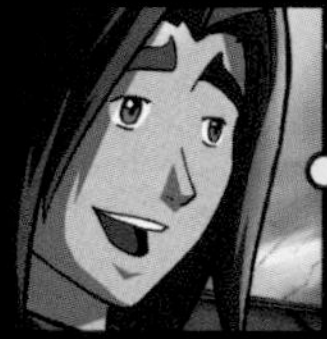

Juston Seyfert
Our Hero

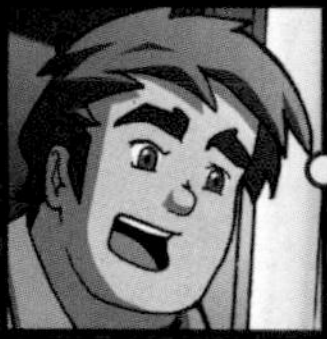

Pete Seyfert
His Dad

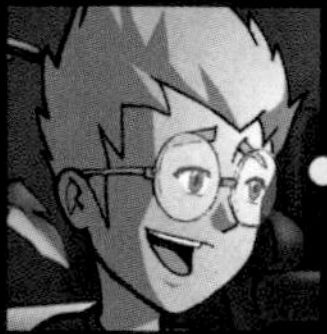

Chris Seyfert
Little Bro

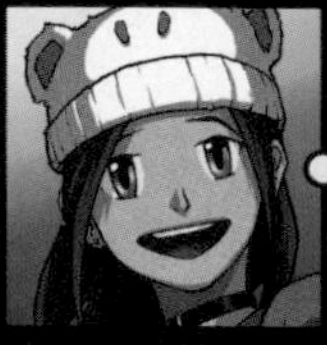

Jessie
The Dream Girl

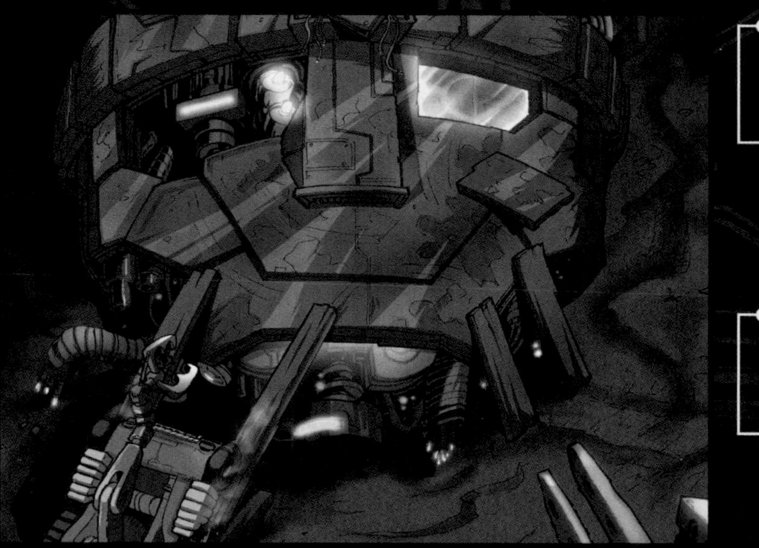

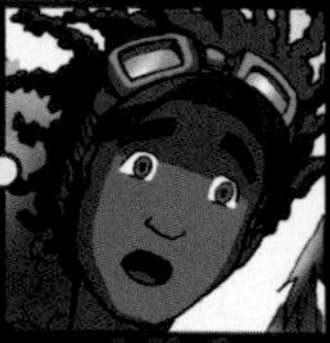

Alex
Best Friend, Part 1

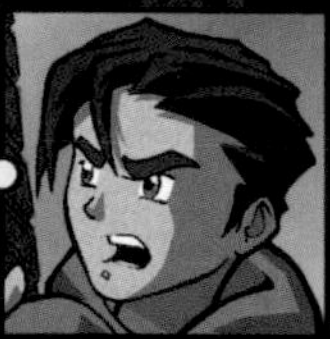

Matt
Best Friend, the Sequel

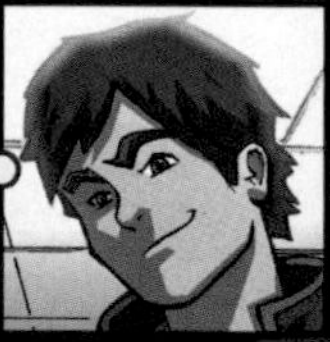

Josh
The Bully

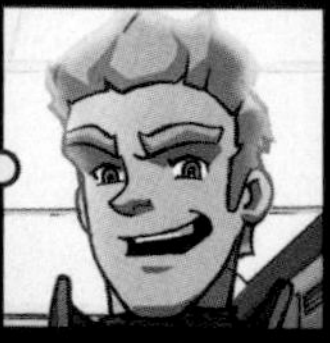

Greg
See "Josh", add Blond

It sucks to be Juston Seyfert. He's tormented by the Seniors at Antigo High School. He has no luck with the ladies. He's dirt poor. He lives in his father's junkyard. And his mother walked out on him and his family years ago. Yeah..."sucks" would be the word.

Without the cash for standard teenage pursuits, Juston builds his own fun—in the form of homemade battlebots that he, his little brother Chris and his friends Matt and Alex compete with.

After finding what looked like a robotic control chip in the salvage yard, Juston decided to install it in his battlebot to see what would happen...and the battlebot zoomed crazily away into the vast fields of junk behind the family house, not to be found again!

But little does Juston realize that his battlebot has made a discovery of its own: a gigantic battle-damaged robot head that—thanks to the battlebot's new control chip—it has begun to repair...

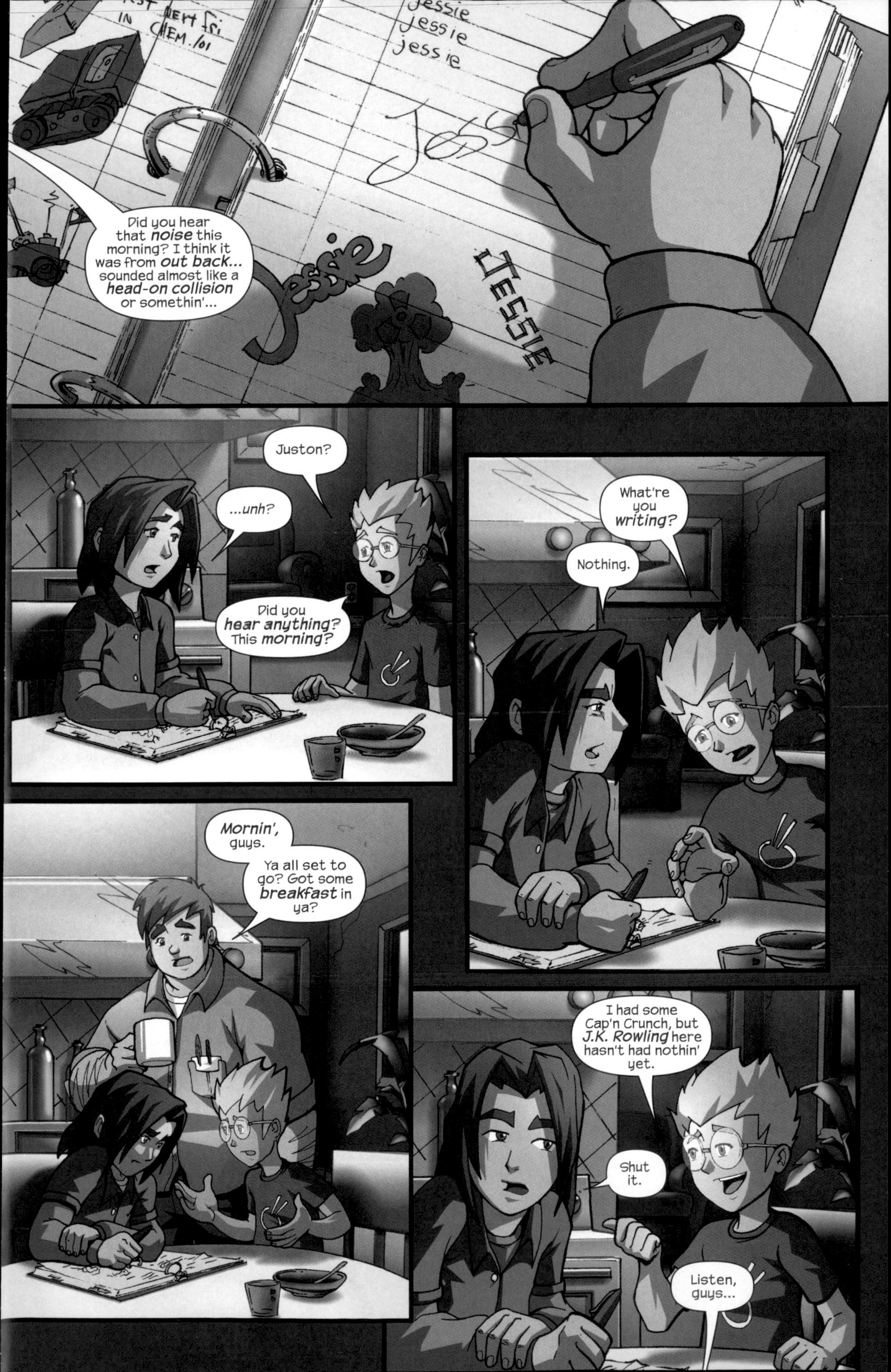

Jessie
jessie
jessie
Did you hear that *noise* this morning? I think it was from *out back...* sounded almost like a *head-on collision* or somethin'...
Jessie
JESSIE
Juston?
...unh?
Did you *hear anything?* This *morning?*
What're you *writing?*
Nothing.
Mornin', guys.
Ya all set to go? Got some *breakfast* in ya?
I had some Cap'n Crunch, but *J.K. Rowling* here hasn't had nothin' yet.
Shut it.
Listen, guys...

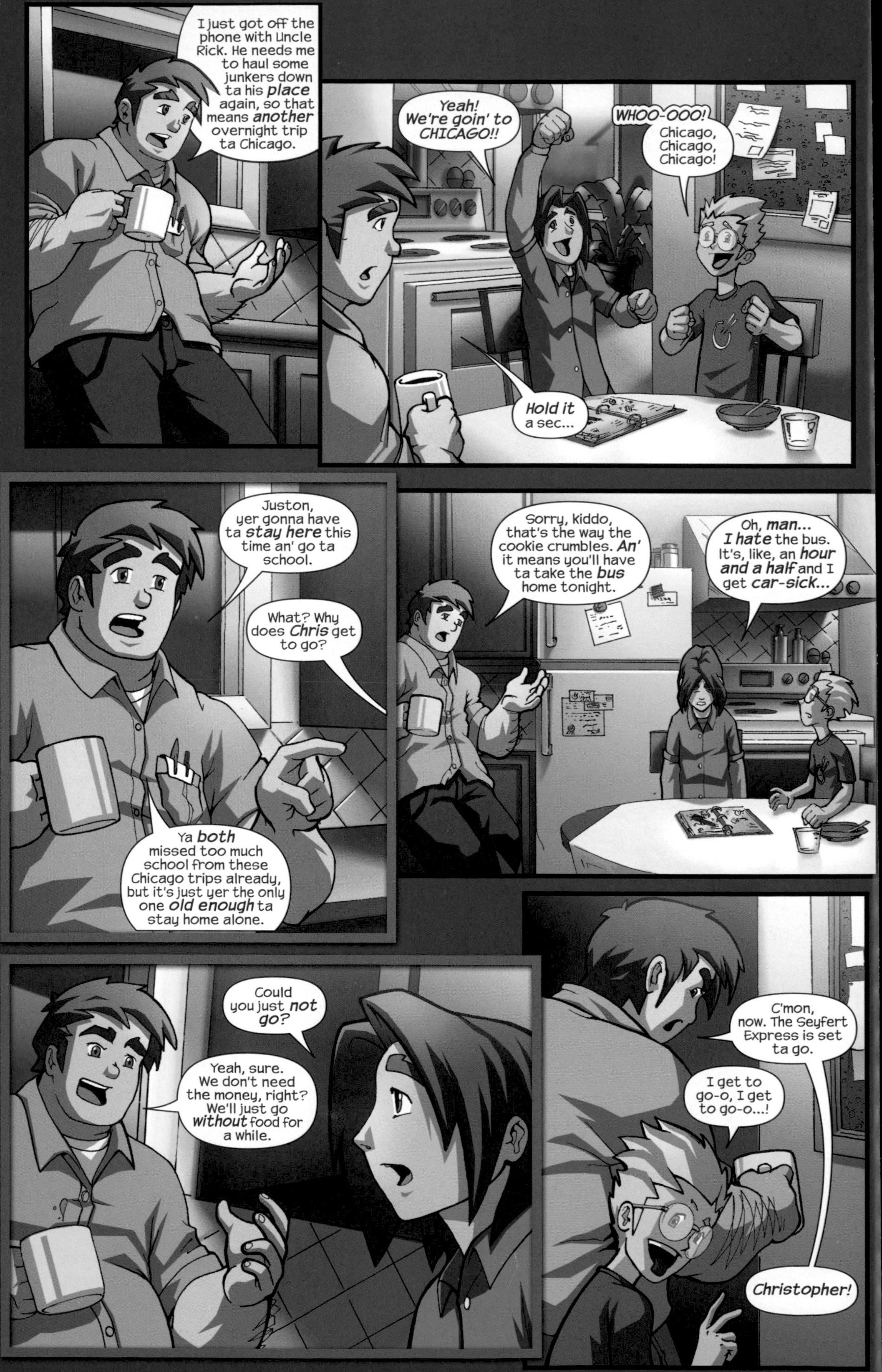

I just got off the phone with Uncle Rick. He needs me to haul some junkers down ta his *place* again, so that means *another* overnight trip ta Chicago.
Yeah! *We're goin' to CHICAGO!!*
WHOO-OOO! Chicago, Chicago, Chicago!
Hold it a sec...
Juston, yer gonna have ta *stay here* this time an' go ta school.
What? Why does *Chris* get to go?
Ya *both* missed too much school from these Chicago trips already, but it's just yer the only one *old enough* ta stay home alone.
Sorry, kiddo, that's the way the cookie crumbles. *An'* it means you'll have ta take the *bus* home tonight.
Oh, *man... I hate* the bus. It's, like, an *hour and a half* and I get *car-sick...*
Could you just *not go?*
Yeah, sure. We don't need the money, right? We'll just go *without* food for a while.
C'mon, now. The Seyfert Express is set ta go.
I get to go-o, I get to go-o...!
Christopher!

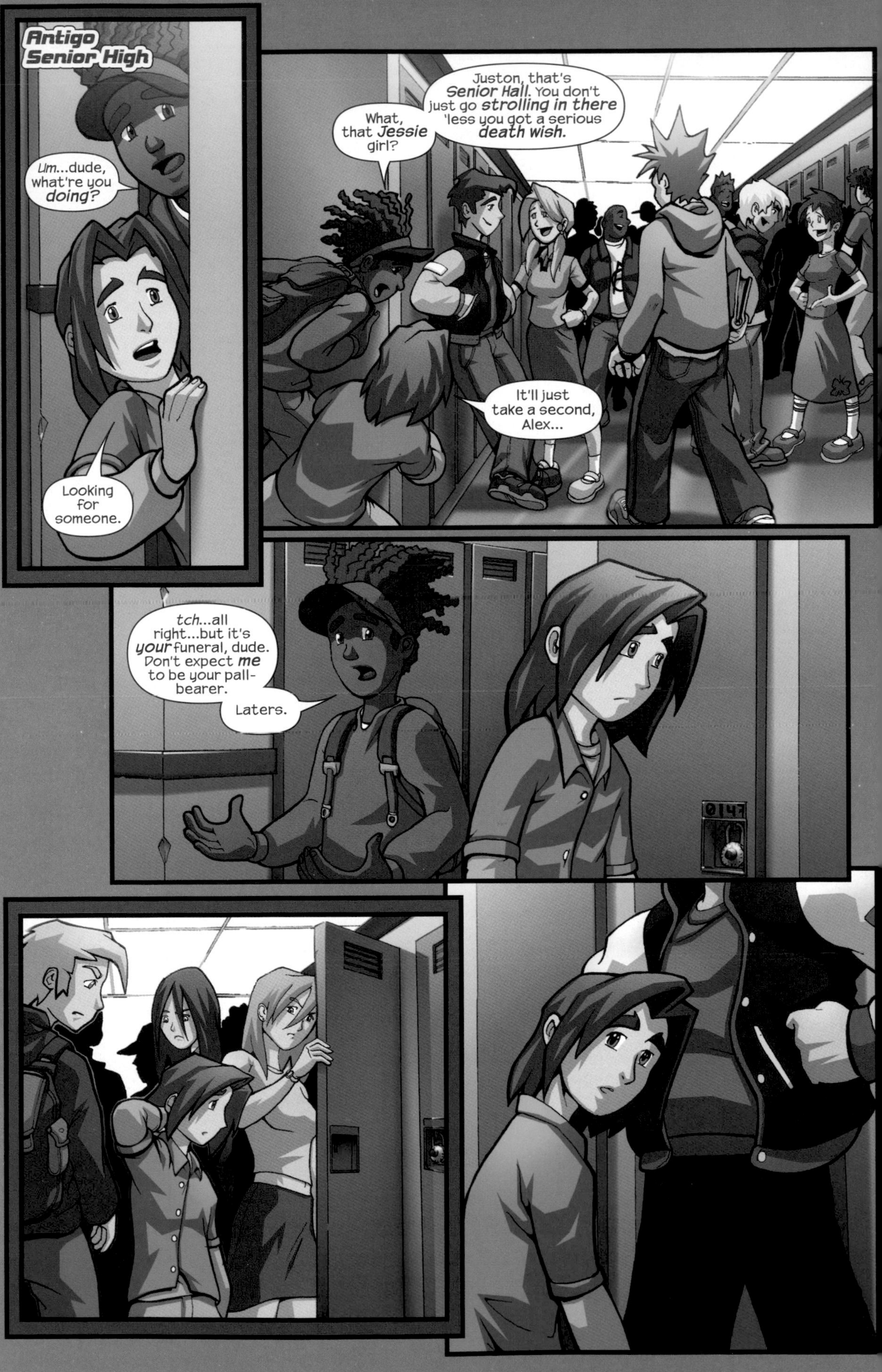
Antigo Senior High
Um...dude, what're you doing?
Looking for someone.
What, that Jessie girl?
Juston, that's Senior Hall. You don't just go strolling in there 'less you got a serious death wish.
It'll just take a second, Alex...
tch...all right...but it's your funeral, dude. Don't expect me to be your pall-bearer.
Laters.

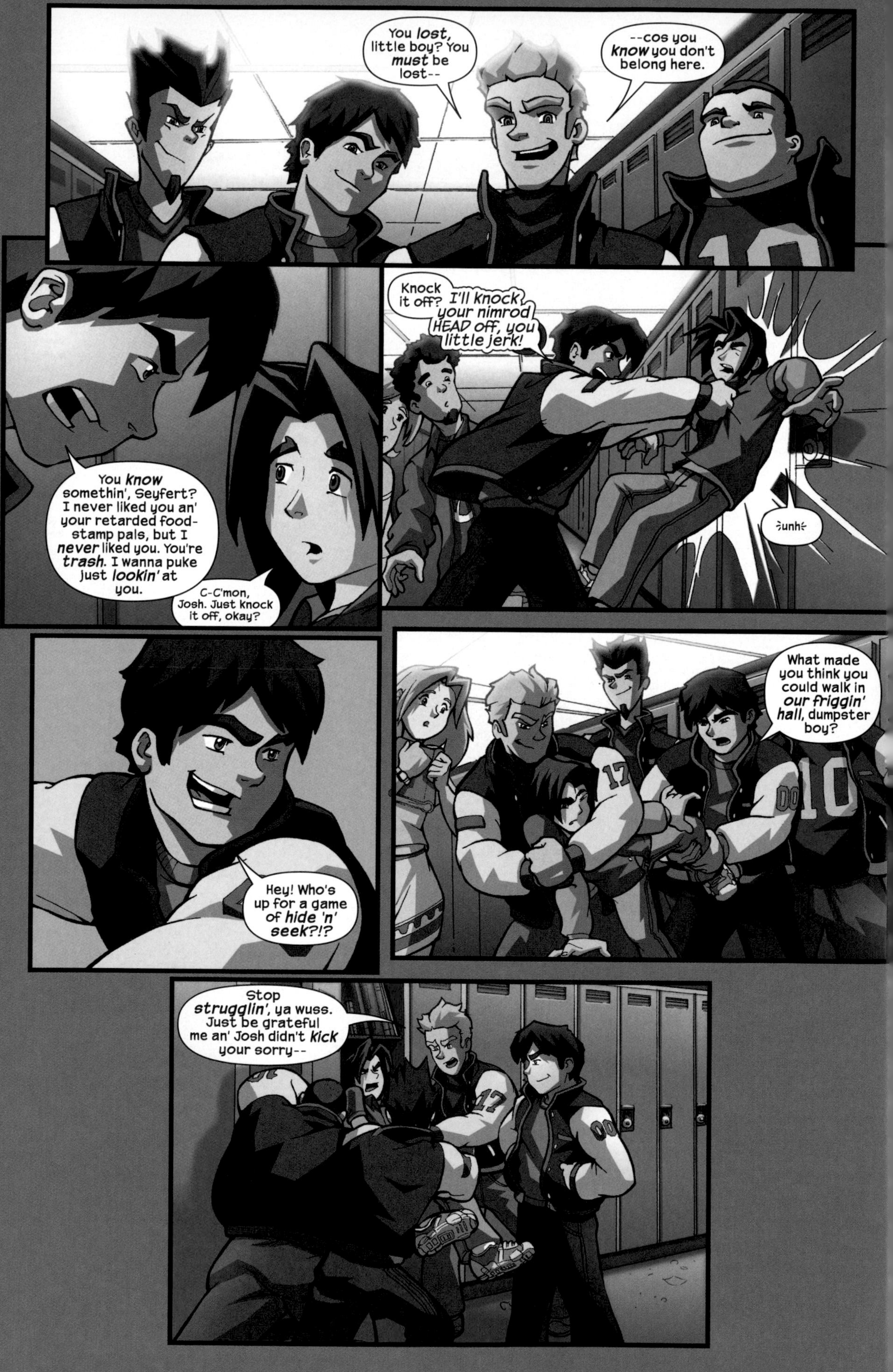
You lost, little boy? You must be lost--
--cos you know you don't belong here.
You know somethin', Seyfert? I never liked you an' your retarded food-stamp pals, but I never liked you. You're trash. I wanna puke just lookin' at you.
C-C'mon, Josh. Just knock it off, okay?
Knock it off?
I'll knock your nimrod HEAD off, you little jerk!
unh
Hey! Who's up for a game of hide 'n' seek?!?
What made you think you could walk in our friggin' hall, dumpster boy?
Stop strugglin', ya wuss. Just be grateful me an' Josh didn't kick your sorry--

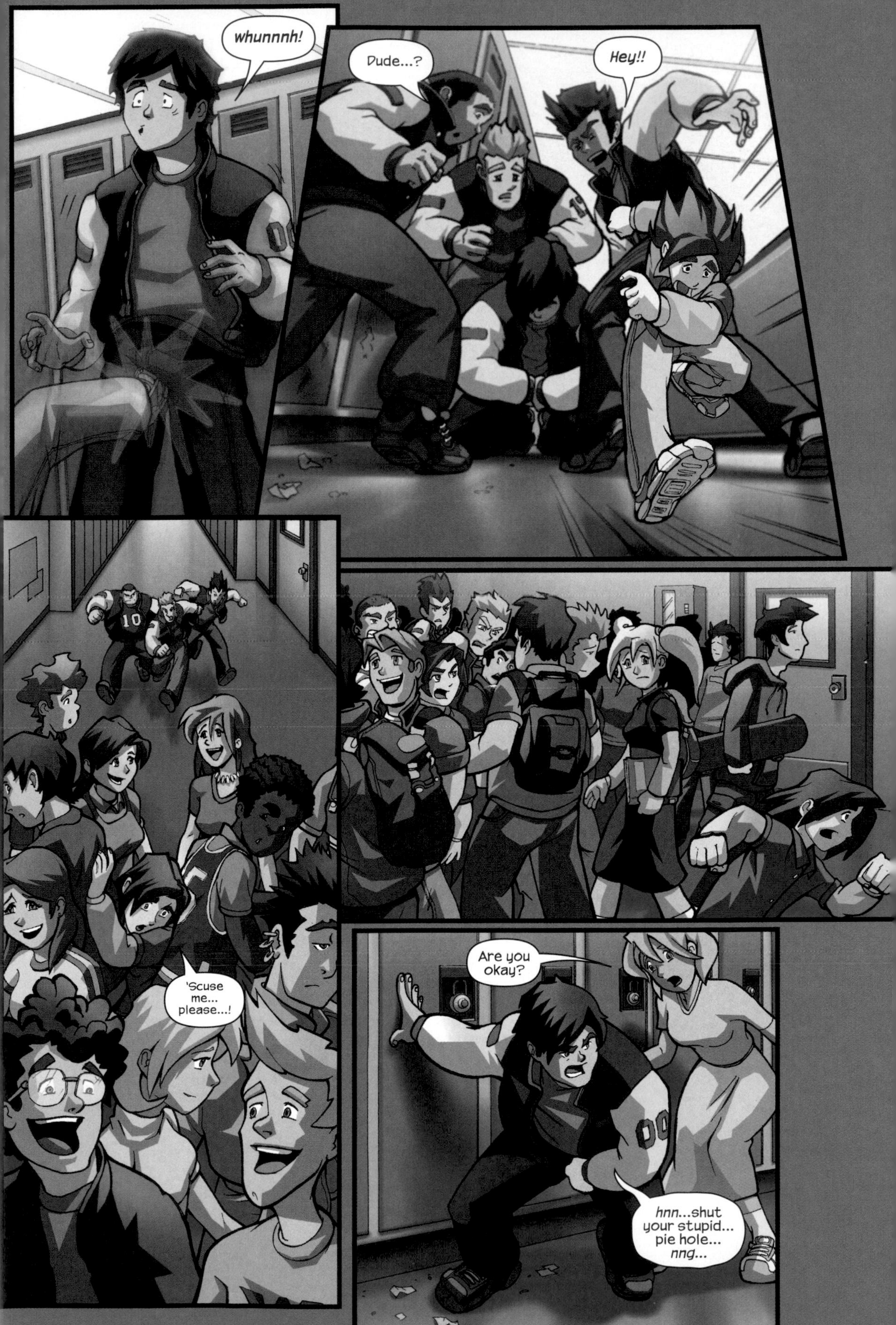
whunnnh!
Dude...?
Hey!!
'Scuse me... please...!
Are you okay?
hnn...shut your stupid... pie hole... nng...

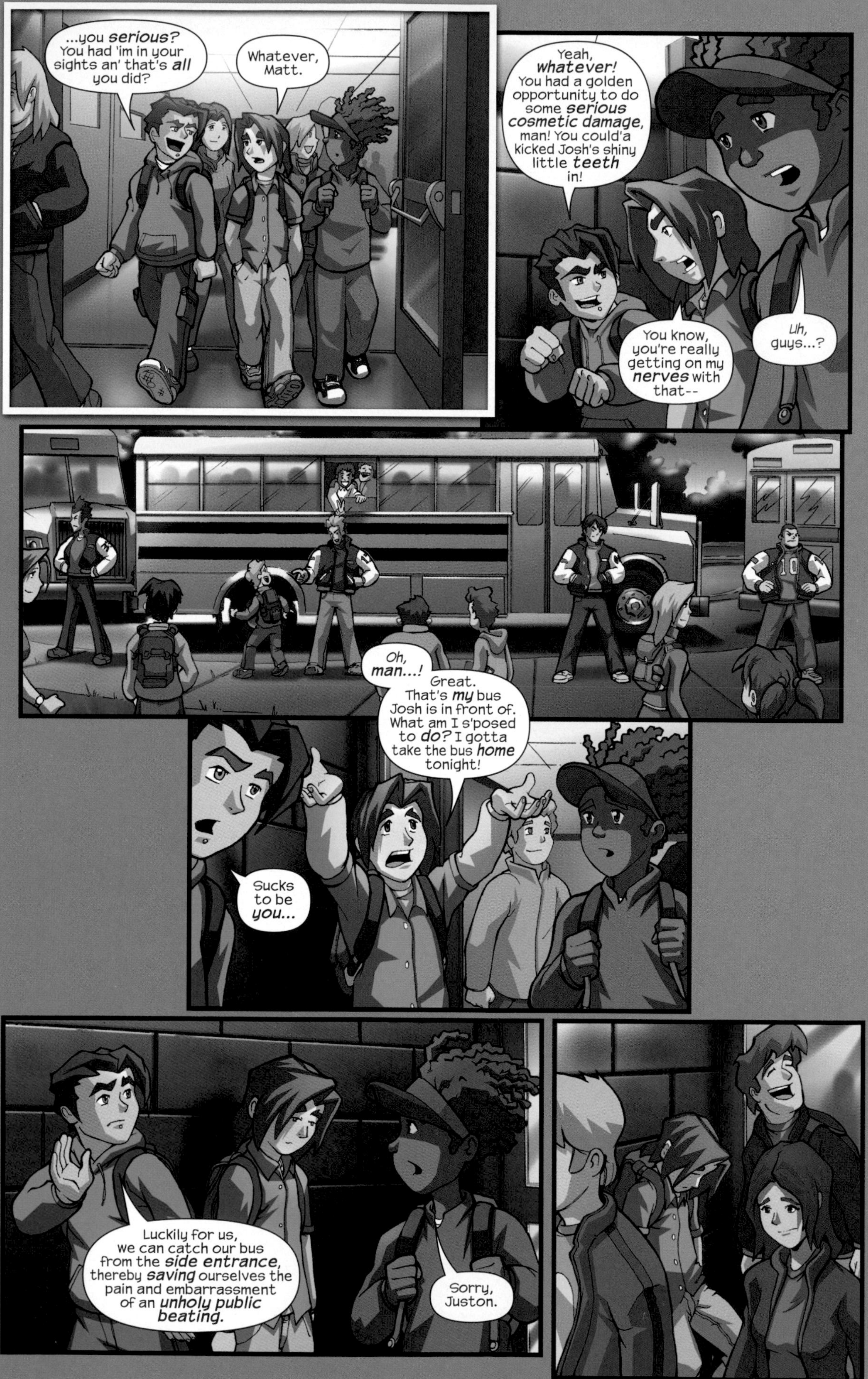
...you serious? You had 'im in your sights an' that's all you did?
Whatever, Matt.
Yeah, whatever! You had a golden opportunity to do some serious cosmetic damage, man! You could'a kicked Josh's shiny little teeth in!
You know, you're really getting on my nerves with that--
Uh, guys...?
Oh, man...!
Great. That's my bus Josh is in front of. What am I s'posed to do? I gotta take the bus home tonight!
Sucks to be you...
Luckily for us, we can catch our bus from the side entrance, thereby saving ourselves the pain and embarrassment of an unholy public beating.
Sorry, Juston.

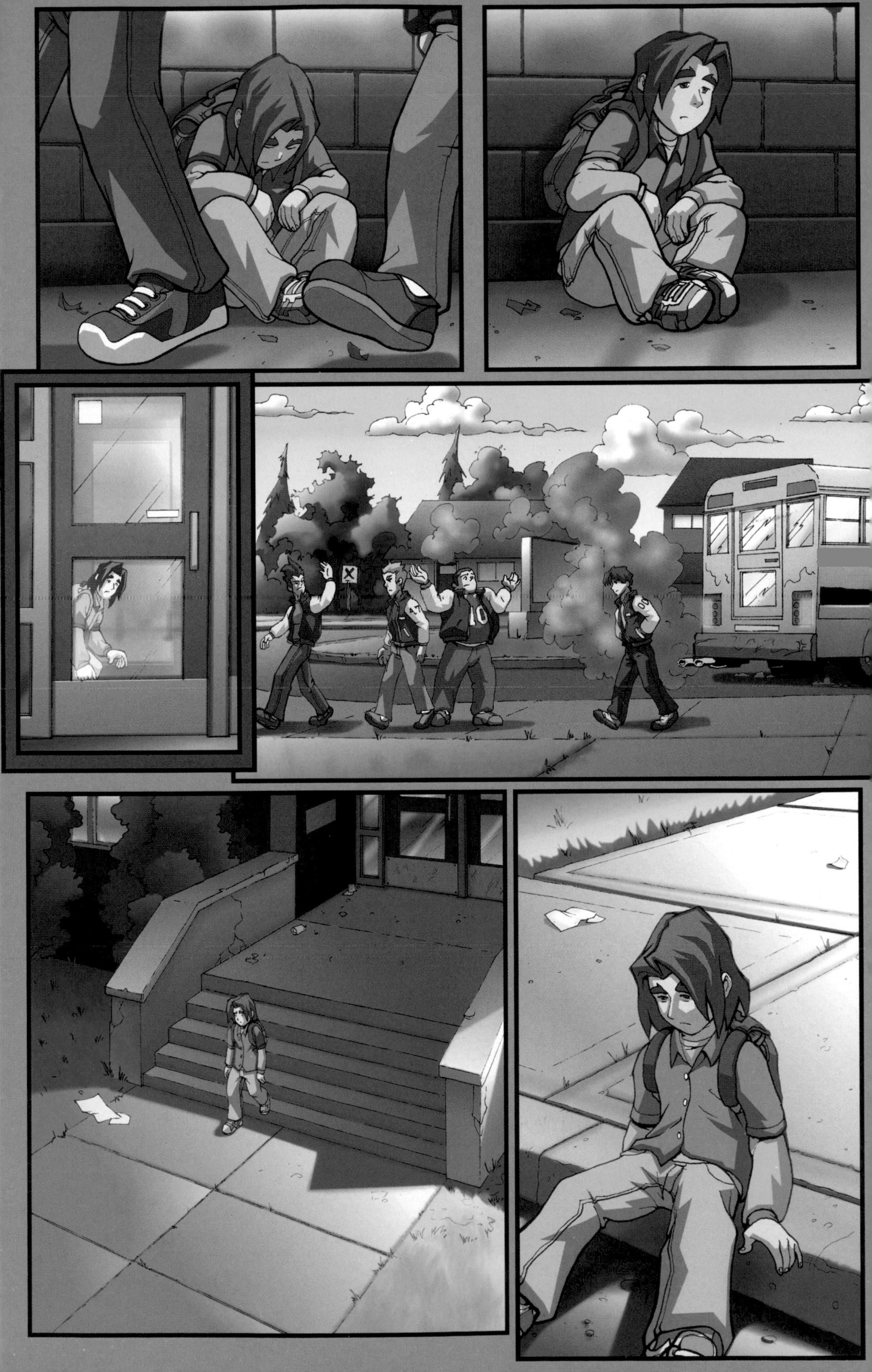

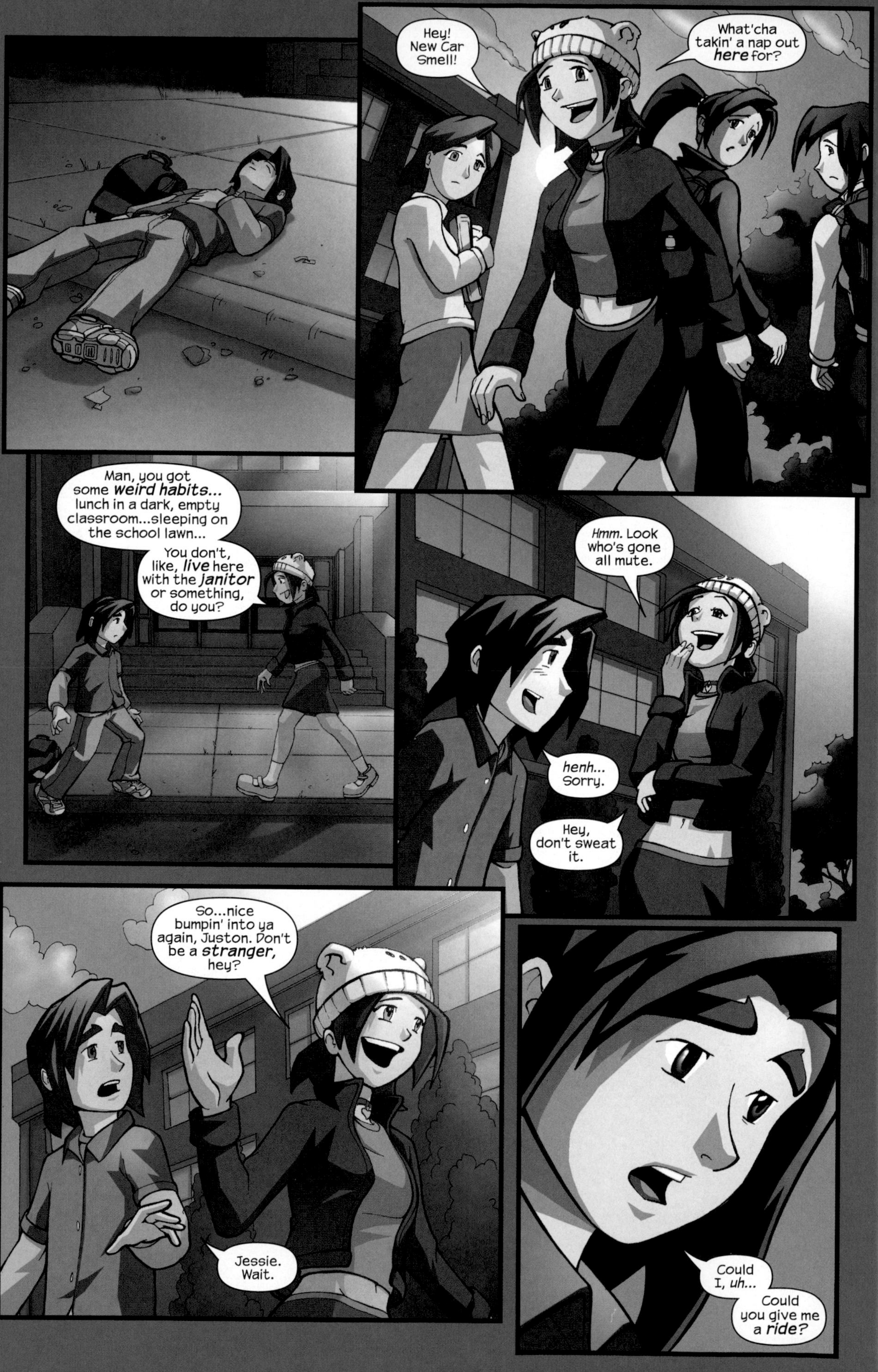
Hey! New Car Smell!
What'cha takin' a nap out here for?
Man, you got some weird habits... lunch in a dark, empty classroom...sleeping on the school lawn...
You don't, like, live here with the janitor or something, do you?
Hmm. Look who's gone all mute.
henh... Sorry.
Hey, don't sweat it.
So...nice bumpin' into ya again, Juston. Don't be a stranger, hey?
Jessie. Wait.
Could I, uh...
Could you give me a ride?

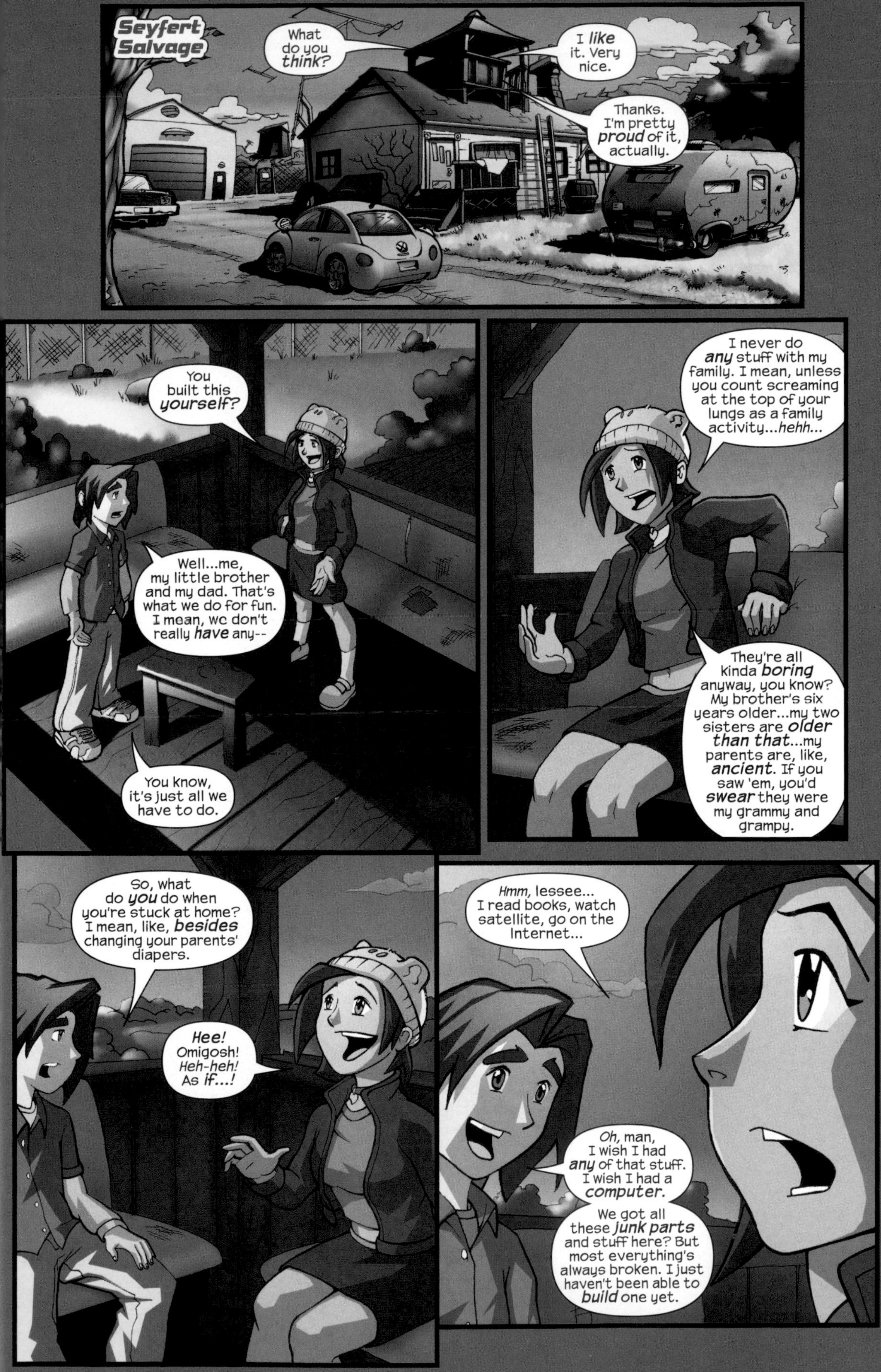
Seyfert Salvage
What do you think?
I like it. Very nice.
Thanks. I'm pretty proud of it, actually.
You built this yourself?
Well...me, my little brother and my dad. That's what we do for fun. I mean, we don't really have any--
You know, it's just all we have to do.
I never do any stuff with my family. I mean, unless you count screaming at the top of your lungs as a family activity...hehh...
They're all kinda boring anyway, you know? My brother's six years older...my two sisters are older than that...my parents are, like, ancient. If you saw 'em, you'd swear they were my grammy and grampy.
So, what do you do when you're stuck at home? I mean, like, besides changing your parents' diapers.
Hee! Omigosh! Heh-heh! As if...!
Hmm, lessee... I read books, watch satellite, go on the Internet...
Oh, man, I wish I had any of that stuff. I wish I had a computer.
We got all these junk parts and stuff here? But most everything's always broken. I just haven't been able to build one yet.

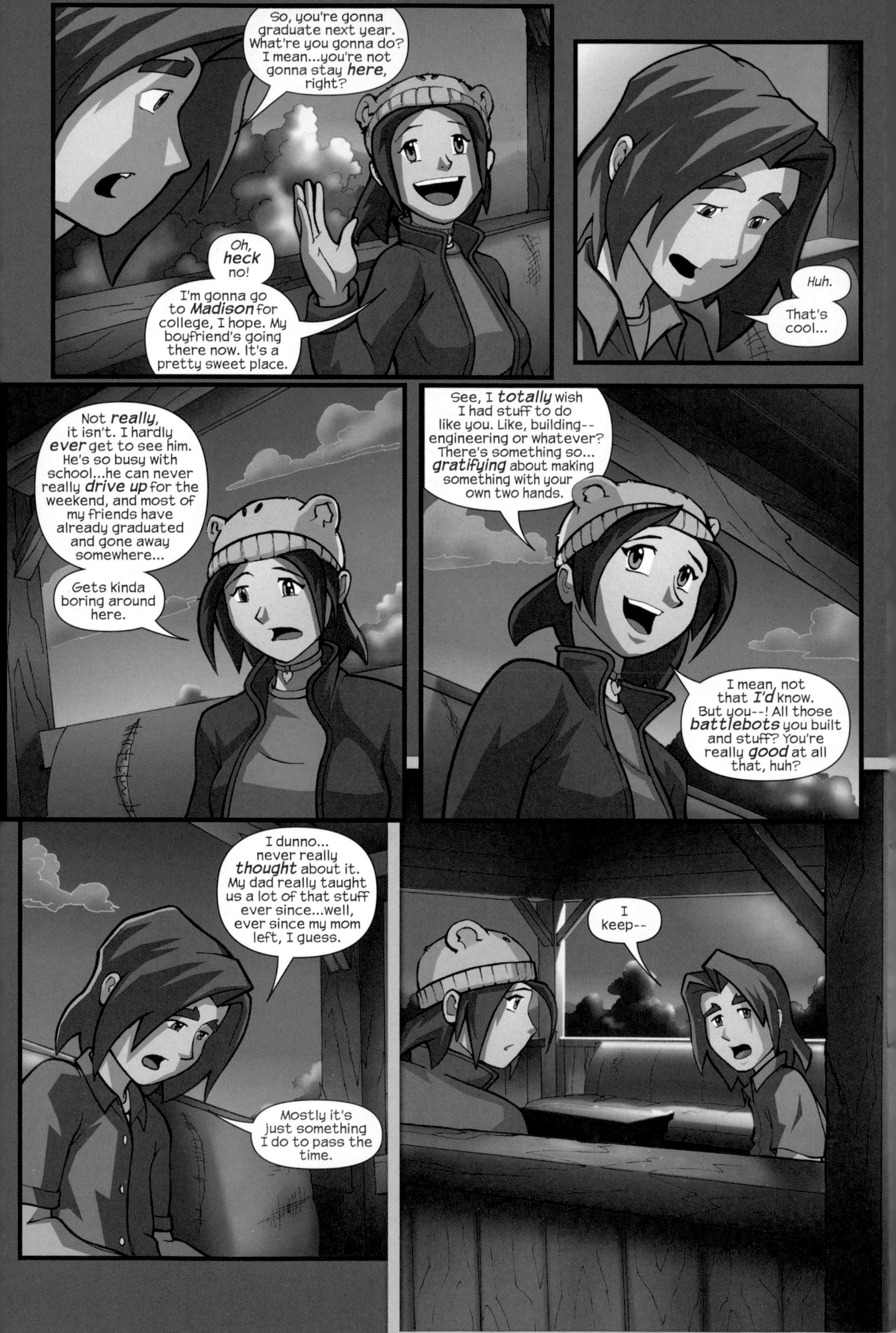

So, you're gonna graduate next year. What're you gonna do? I mean...you're not gonna stay *here*, right?
Oh, *heck* no!
I'm gonna go to *Madison* for college, I hope. My boyfriend's going there now. It's a pretty sweet place.
Huh.
That's cool...
Not *really*, it isn't. I hardly *ever* get to see him. He's so busy with school...he can never really *drive up* for the weekend, and most of my friends have already graduated and gone away somewhere...
Gets kinda boring around here.
See, I *totally* wish I had stuff to do like you. Like, building-- engineering or whatever? There's something so... *gratifying* about making something with your own two hands.
I mean, not that *I'd* know. But you--! All those *battlebots* you built and stuff? You're really *good* at all that, huh?
I dunno... never really *thought* about it. My dad really taught us a lot of that stuff ever since...well, ever since my mom left, I guess.
Mostly it's just something I do to pass the time.
I keep--

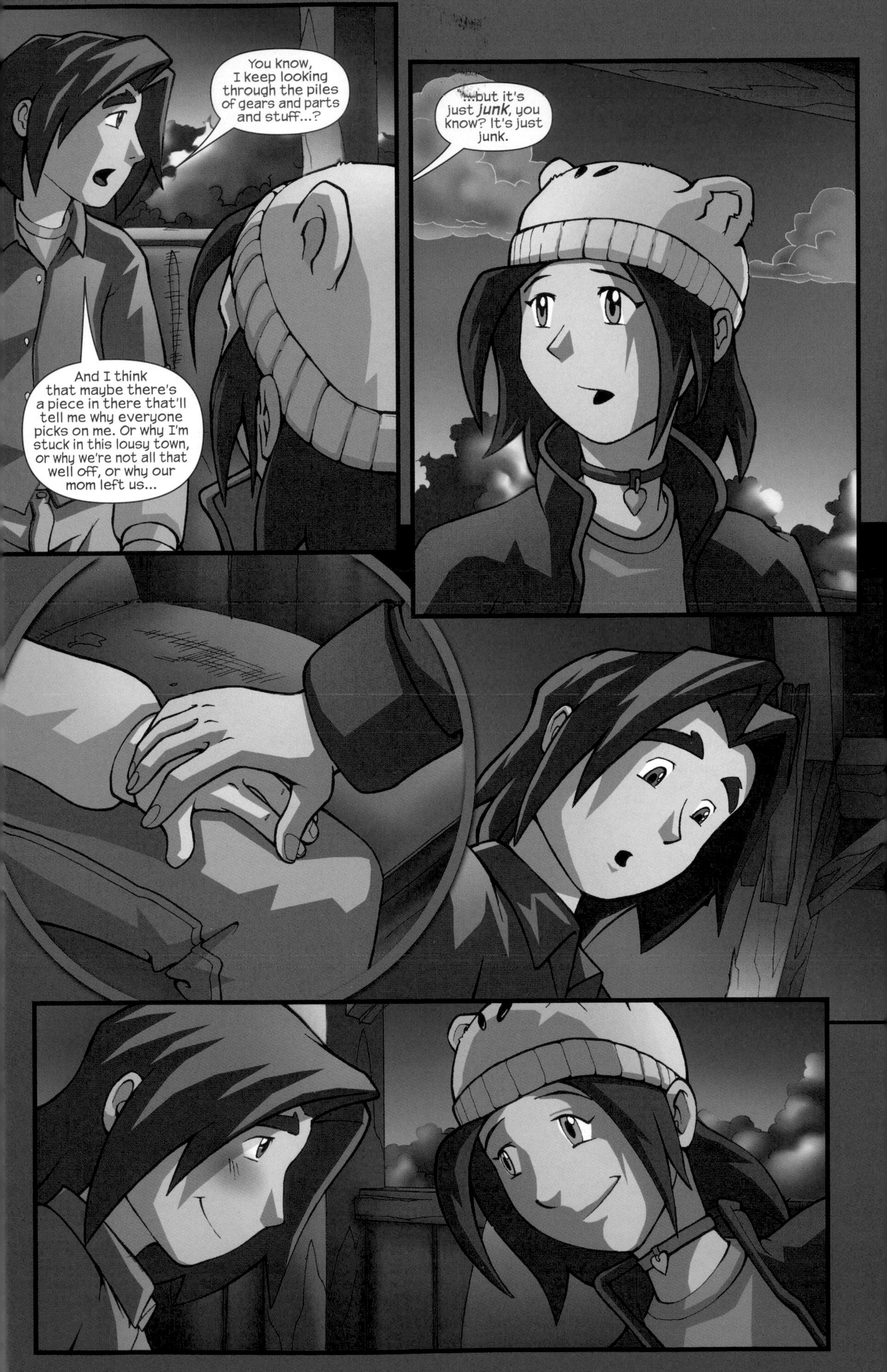
You know, I keep looking through the piles of gears and parts and stuff...?
And I think that maybe there's a piece in there that'll tell me why everyone picks on me. Or why I'm stuck in this lousy town, or why we're not all that well off, or why our mom left us...
...but it's just *junk*, you know? It's just junk.

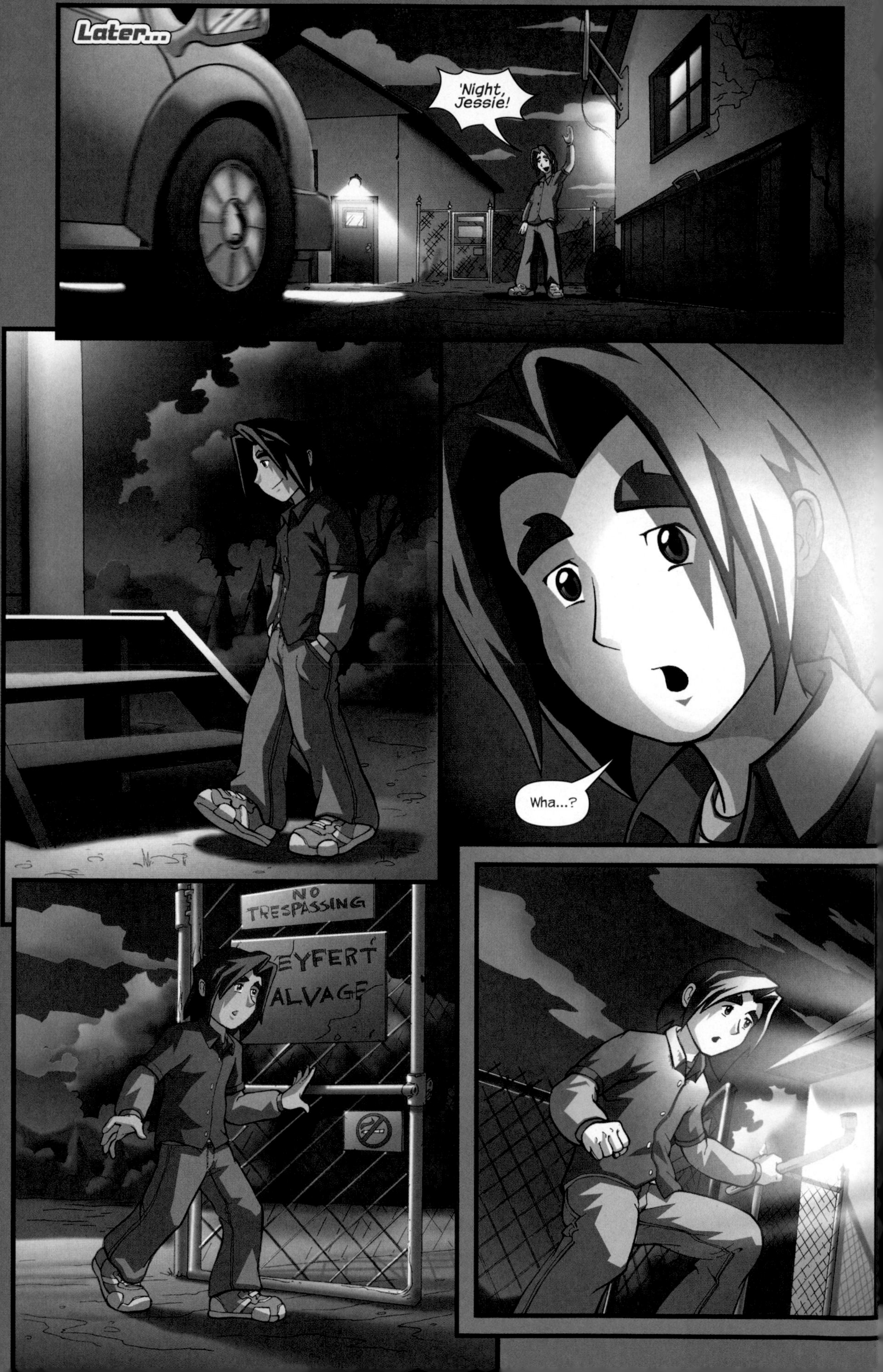

Later...
'Night, Jessie!
Wha...?
NO TRESPASSING
EYFERT
ALVAGE

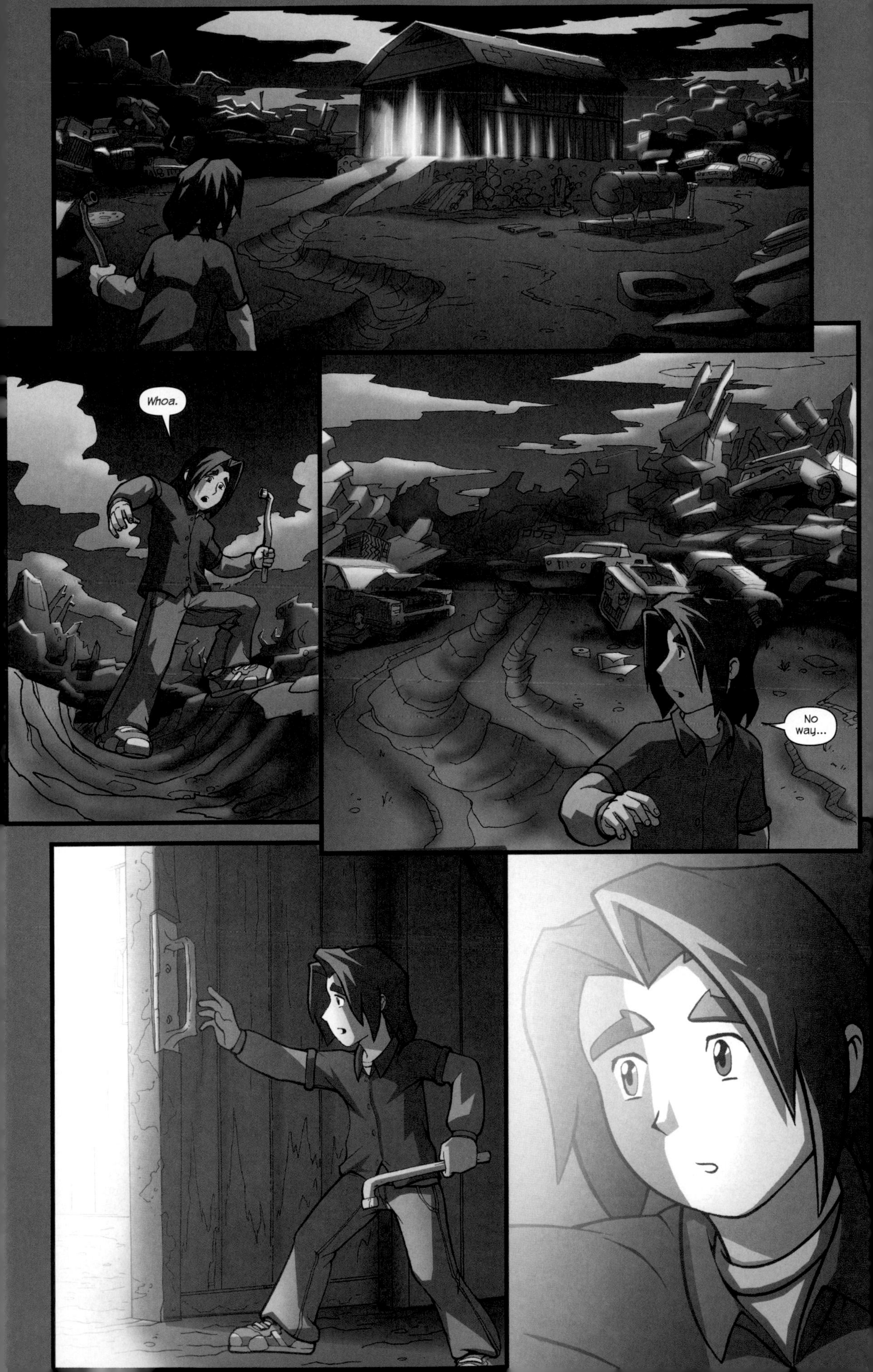
Whoa.
No way...

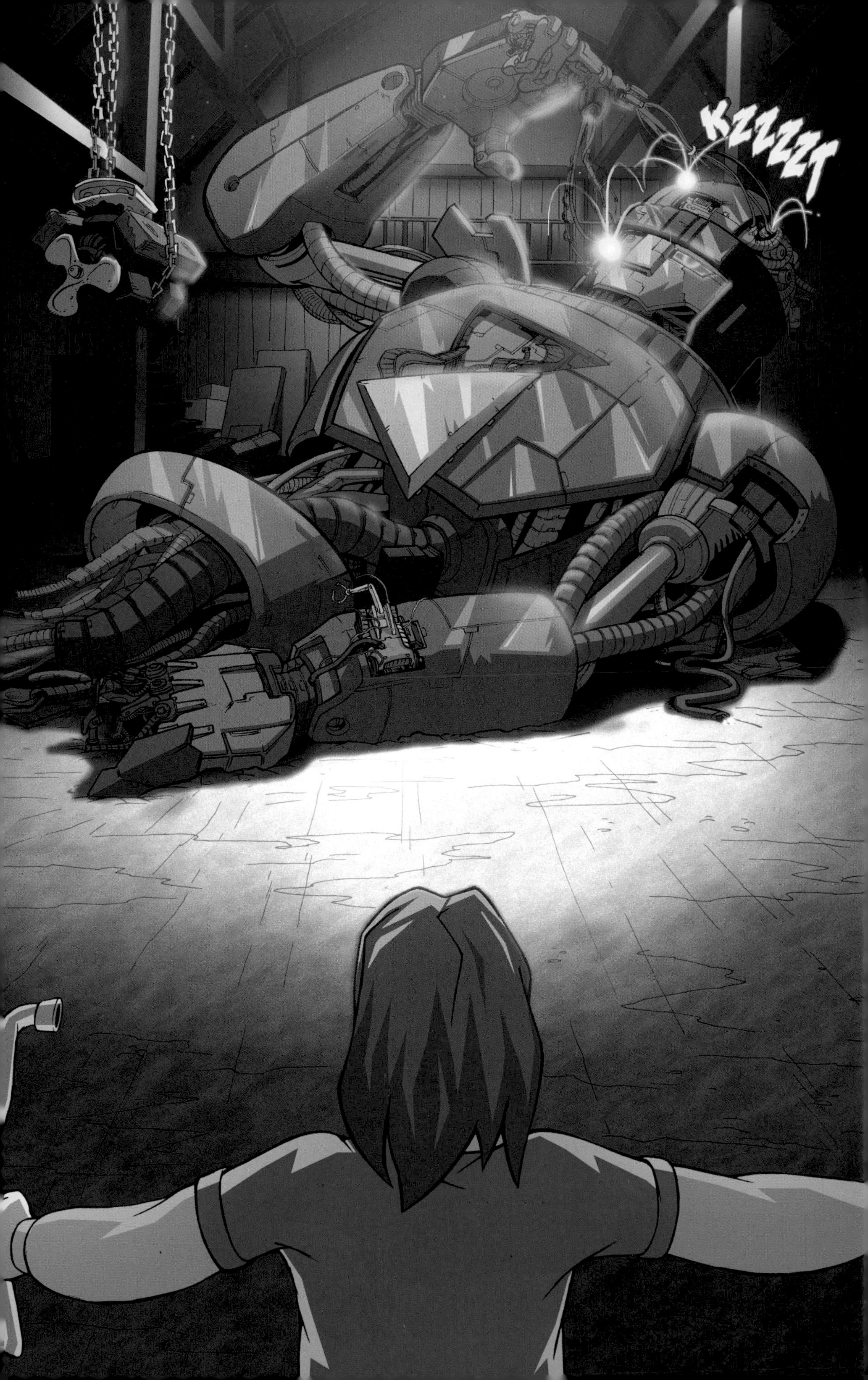
KZZZZZT

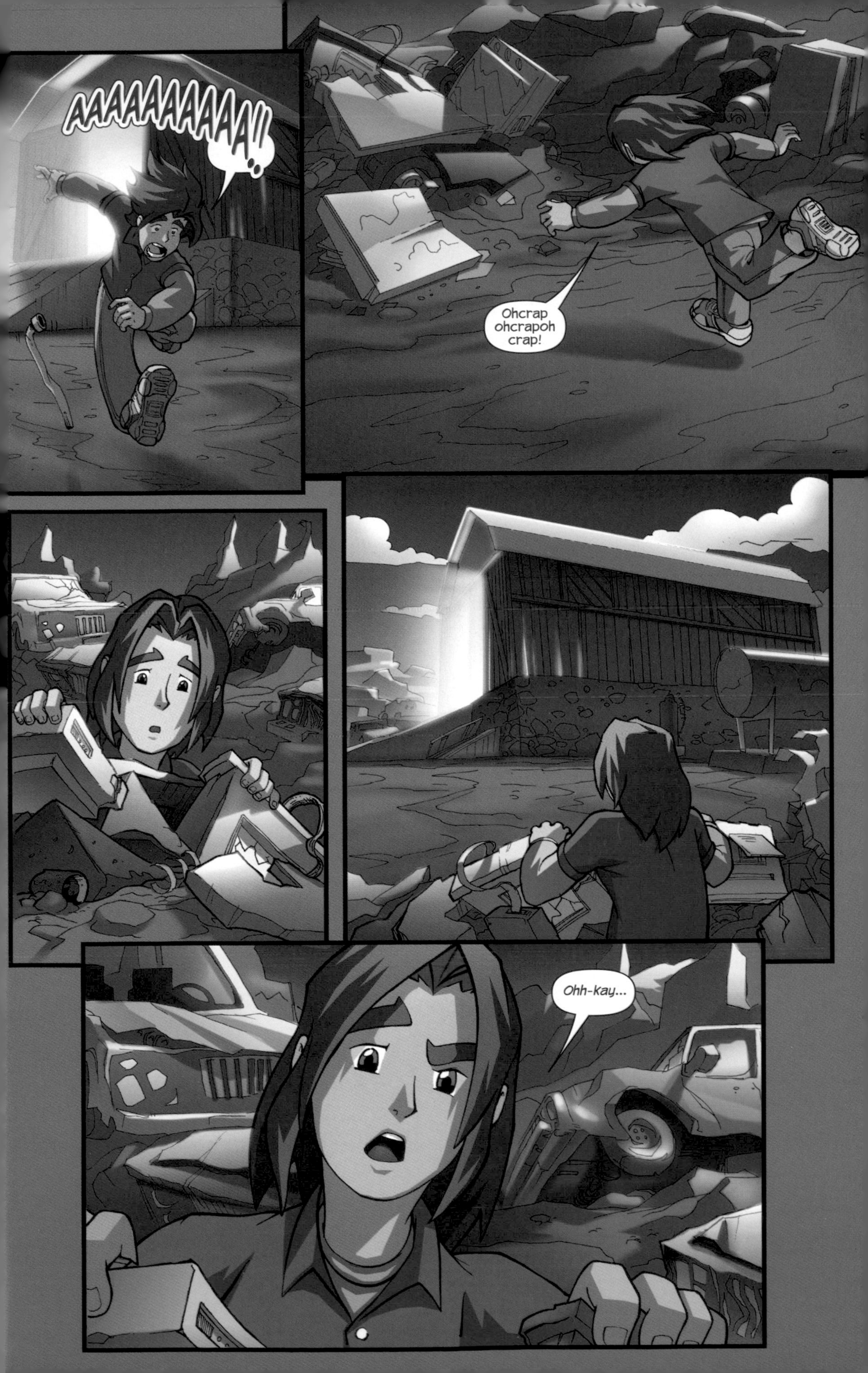
AAAAAAAAAAA!!
Ohcrap ohcrapoh crap!
Ohh-kay...

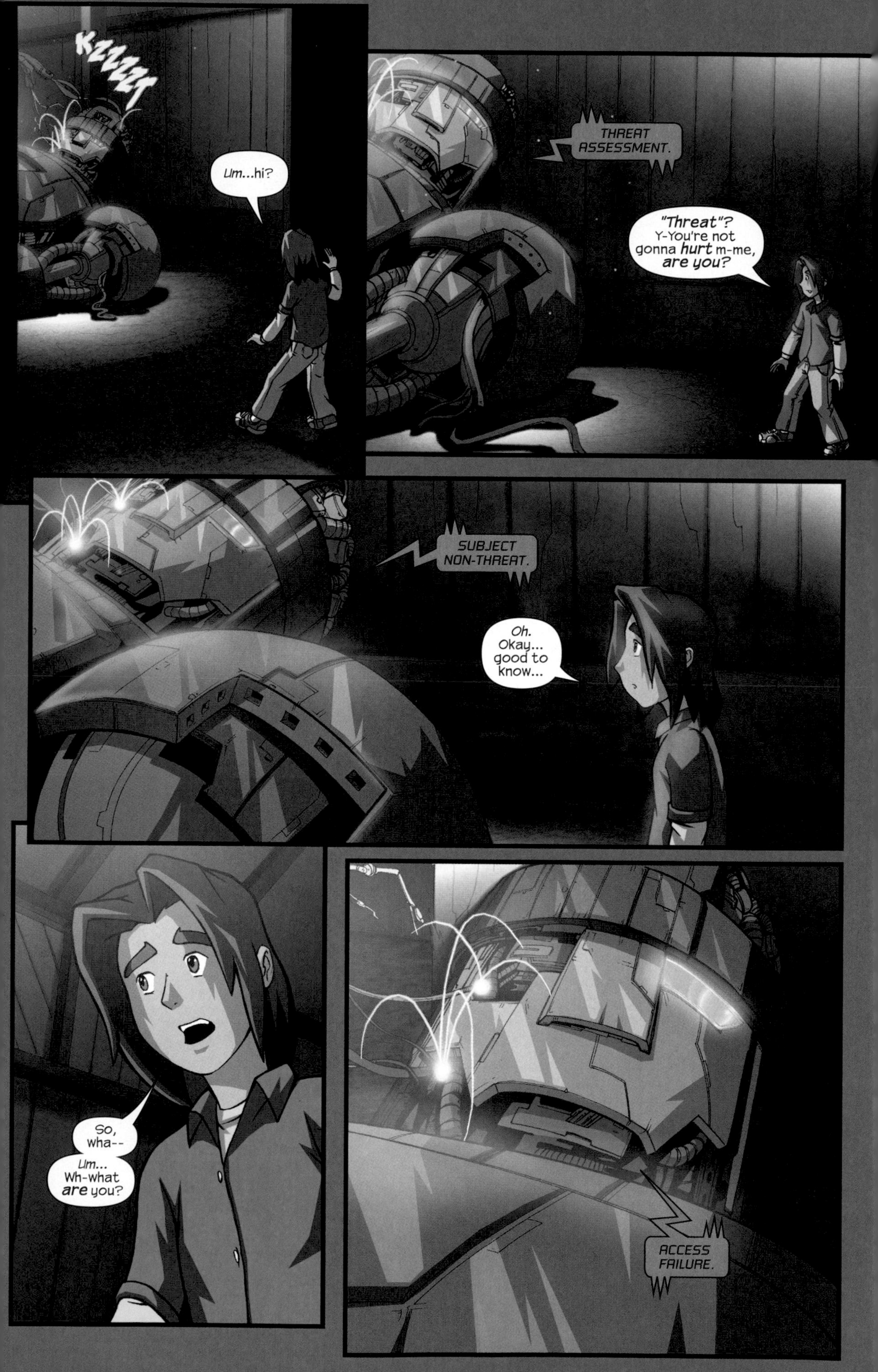
KZZZZT
Um...hi?
THREAT ASSESSMENT.
"Threat"? Y-You're not gonna hurt m-me, are you?
SUBJECT NON-THREAT.
Oh. Okay... good to know...
So, wha--
Um... Wh-what are you?
ACCESS FAILURE.

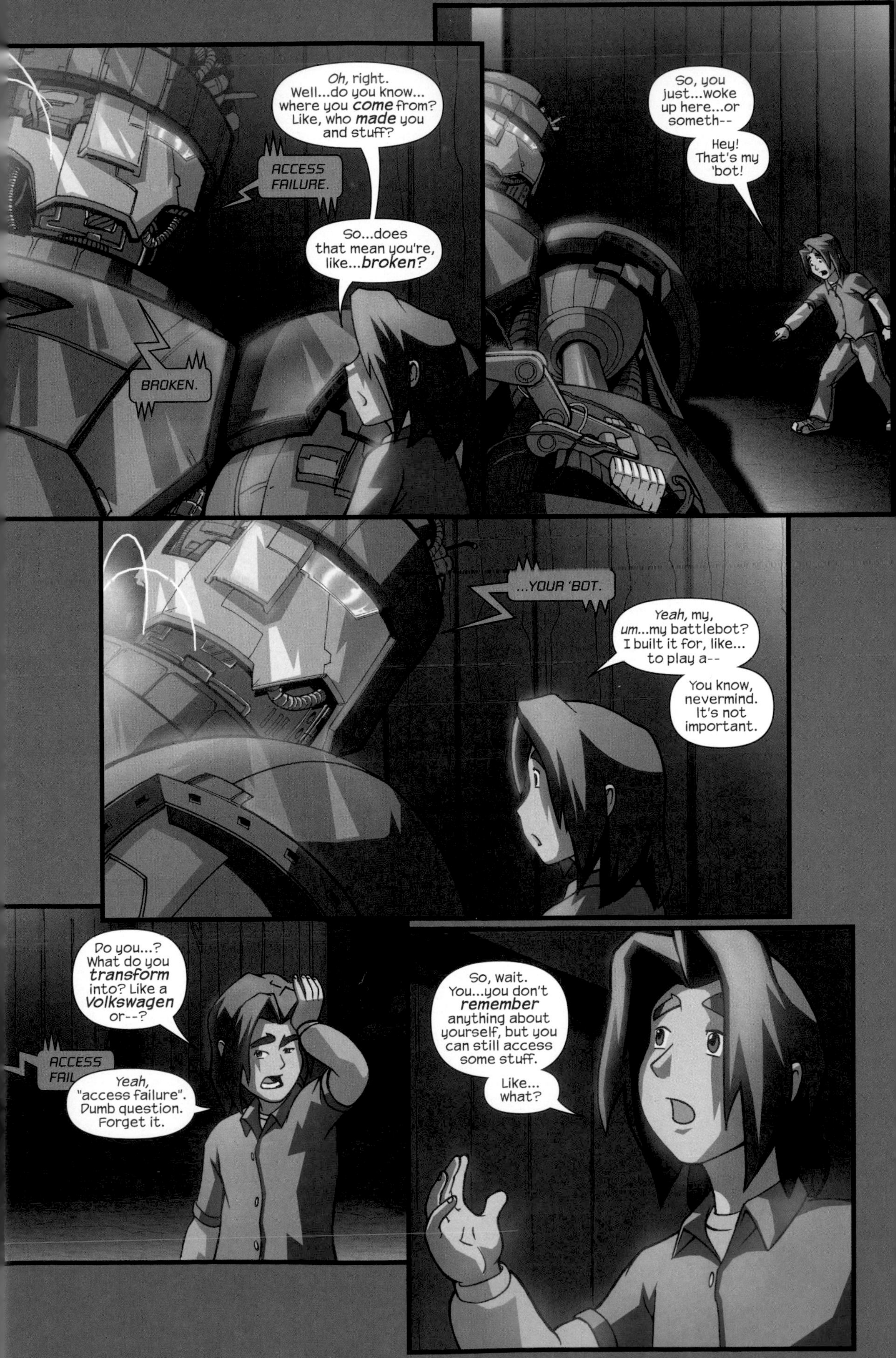
Oh, right. Well...do you know... where you come from? Like, who made you and stuff?
ACCESS FAILURE.
So...does that mean you're, like...broken?
BROKEN.
So, you just...woke up here...or someth--
Hey! That's my 'bot!
...YOUR 'BOT.
Yeah, my, um...my battlebot? I built it for, like... to play a--
You know, nevermind. It's not important.
Do you...? What do you transform into? Like a Volkswagen or--?
ACCESS FAIL
Yeah, "access failure". Dumb question. Forget it.
So, wait. You...you don't remember anything about yourself, but you can still access some stuff.
Like... what?

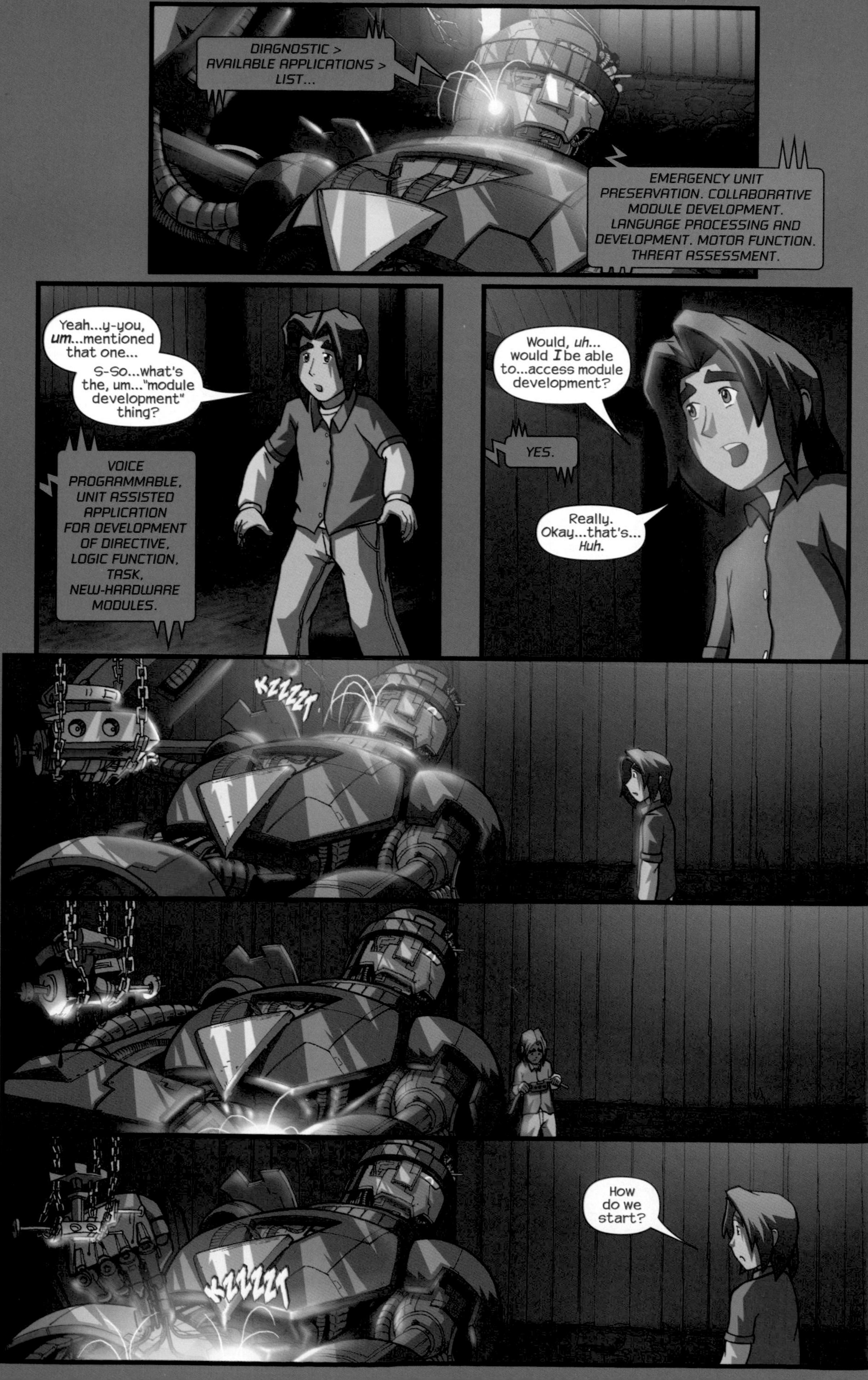
DIAGNOSTIC > AVAILABLE APPLICATIONS > LIST...
EMERGENCY UNIT PRESERVATION. COLLABORATIVE MODULE DEVELOPMENT. LANGUAGE PROCESSING AND DEVELOPMENT. MOTOR FUNCTION. THREAT ASSESSMENT.
Yeah...y-you, um...mentioned that one...
S-So...what's the, um..."module development" thing?
VOICE PROGRAMMABLE, UNIT ASSISTED APPLICATION FOR DEVELOPMENT OF DIRECTIVE, LOGIC FUNCTION, TASK, NEW-HARDWARE MODULES.
Would, uh... would I be able to...access module development?
YES.
Really. Okay...that's... Huh.
KZZZZT
How do we start?
KZZZZT

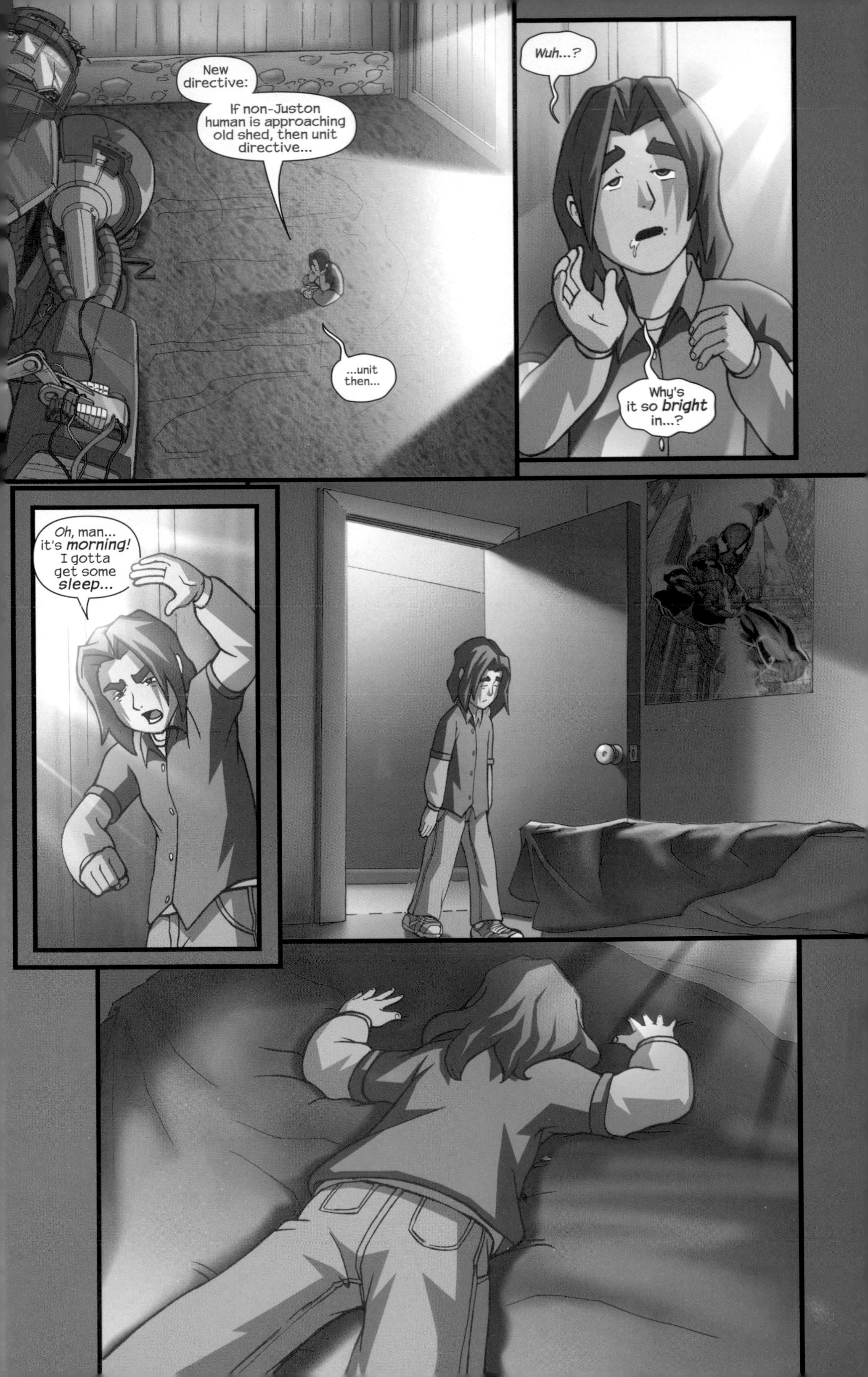
New directive:
If non-Juston human is approaching old shed, then unit directive...
...unit then...
Wuh...?
Why's it so bright in...?
Oh, man... it's morning! I gotta get some sleep...

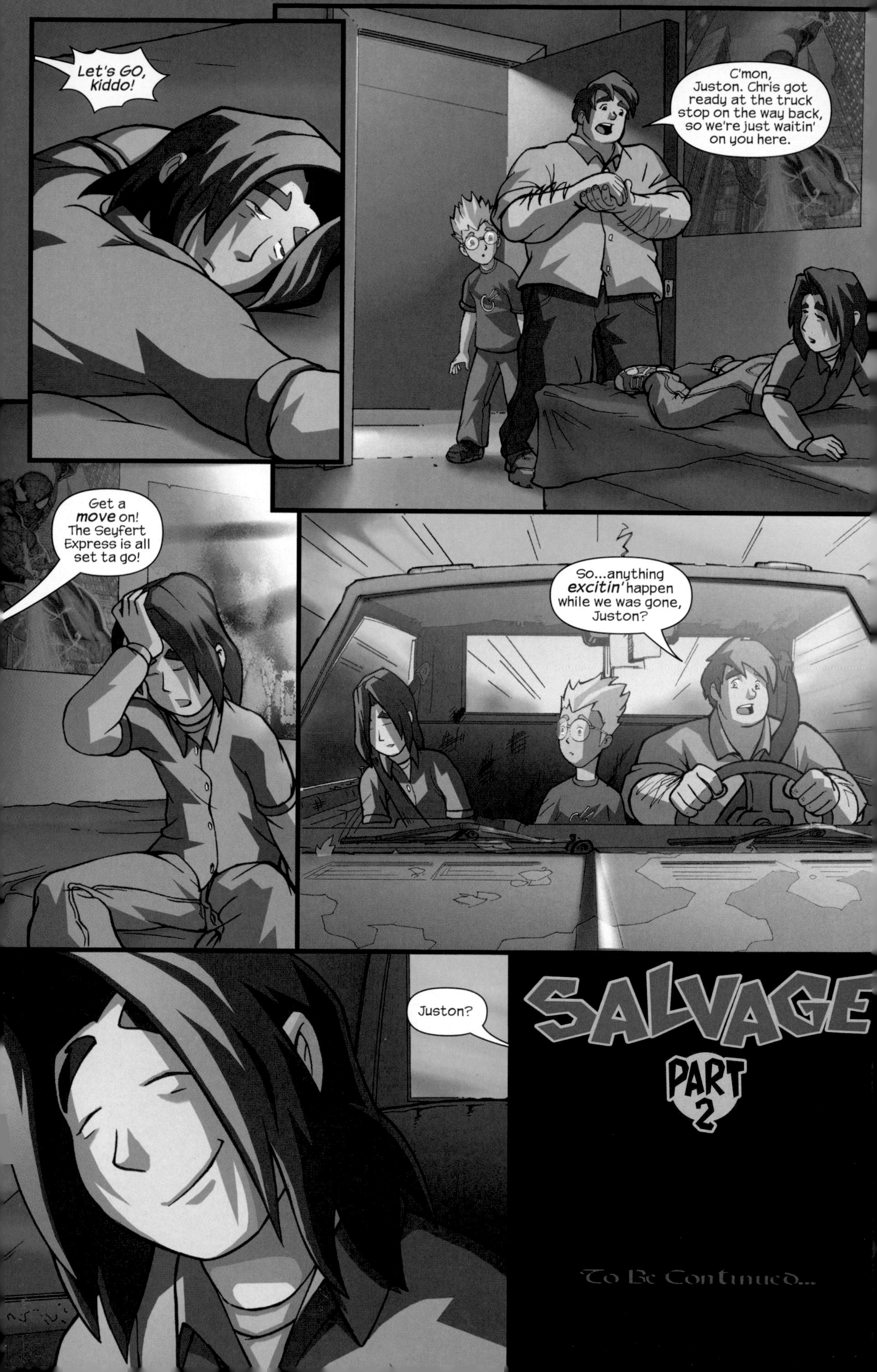
Let's GO, kiddo!
C'mon, Juston. Chris got ready at the truck stop on the way back, so we're just waitin' on you here.
Get a move on! The Seyfert Express is all set ta go!
So...anything excitin' happen while we was gone, Juston?
Juston?
SALVAGE
PART 2
To Be Continued...